The
GYPSY PRINCESS

Phoebe Gilman

Scholastic Press/New York

The illustrations for this book were built up
in layers of oil and egg tempera on gessoed watercolor paper.
This layered technique is
what gives the colors their luminosity.
The paintings were done at twice the size of the book
to allow extra detail to be added.

Library of Congress Cataloging-in-Publication Data

Gilman, Phoebe
The gypsy princess / Phoebe Gilman.
p. cm.
Summary: A gypsy girl who gets the opportunity to live in a
palace as a princess finds she prefers her gypsy life after all.
ISBN 0-590-86543-9
[1. Gypsies—Fiction. 2. Princesses—Fiction.]
I. Title.
PZ7.G4335Gy   1997
[E]—dc20   96-25927
CIP
AC

12 11 10 9 8 7 6 5 4 3 2 1   7 8 9/9 0 1 2/0

Printed in Singapore   46
First American printing, March 1997

*With love for
Michael-Laurie.*

There once was a wild gypsy girl who dreamed of being a princess. She lived in a gypsy caravan and her name was Cinnamon.

Cinnamon knew many things. She could read your fortune in a crystal ball. She knew where to find herbs in the forest and how to brew them into strange potions. She could speak to the wind and she knew how to dance with a bear.

But she wanted to dance with a prince.

In the evenings, after supper, she would sit by the open fire listening to her old auntie tell tales of magic and enchantment. Tales of mermaids and pirates, of dragons and princesses.

"Oh," Cinnamon sighed, "if only I could live in a palace like Princess Cyprina."

"Even a princess can be unhappy," her old auntie replied.

"Impossible," Cinnamon said, as she whittled a piece of wood she had found in the forest.

The old gypsy woman smiled with pleasure as she watched Cinnamon free another creature from its prison of wood. "There are things more precious than a crown of gold," she said.

Cinnamon didn't believe her.

One day, Princess Cyprina came to the gypsy caravan to have her fortune told. Cinnamon gazed into the crystal ball and her eyes grew wide. "I see a great palace. I see a handsome prince. I see diamonds, rubies, pearls…great fortune!"

Princess Cyprina laughed merrily, then opened her purse and dropped a silver coin into Cinnamon's outstretched palm. "They tell me you dance with a bear, gypsy girl. I should like to see that."

"I will try," Cinnamon said, "but Babalatzzi does not always feel like dancing."

Cinnamon picked up her tambourine and began to sing a wild gypsy song:

Ba-ba-latzzi, Babalatzzi,
Come and dance a step or two.
Ba-ba-latzzi, Babalatzzi,
I would love to dance with you.

Babalatzzi came, and Babalatzzi danced.

"What fun!" said the princess, clapping her hands. "You and your bear must come back to my palace. We will play together and I shall never be bored again."

Babalatzzi shook his head. He would not go.

But Cinnamon scarcely hesitated. She kissed her old auntie, waved goodbye to Babalatzzi and the gypsies and climbed into the royal carriage.

Princess Cyprina declared, "From this day forth you shall be known as Princess Cinnamon."

And she was.

Royal handmaids bathed her with scented water. They combed her wild dark hair and set it with a heavy pomade. They dressed her in a gown of satin, embroidered with precious jewels and suspended over seven crinolines.

Cinnamon looked in the gilded palace mirror and barely recognized the girl looking back at her.

At first, the two princesses played happily together. Princess Cinnamon sat upon an ebony horse with tinkling tassels and sapphire eyes while Princess Cyprina showed her many wonderful princess toys.

Every morning, royal handmaids combed and pomaded Cinnamon's princess hairdo. Every evening, she danced with princes in the grand palace ballroom.

"Isn't this fun?" Princess Cyprina called out as she danced past.

Cinnamon's feet were pinched and sore from the beautiful high-heeled princess shoes she wore. She wanted to tell Princess Cyprina that it was more fun to dance with Babalatzzi, but she never had the chance. Princess Cyprina had swirled out of sight.

As the days passed into weeks, the wonderful princess toys no longer seemed so wonderful. Each time they were wound, they did exactly what they had done the time before.

"Where are the dragons and mermaids?" Cinnamon asked.

Princess Cyprina tapped a dainty foot upon the marble palace floor. "Don't ask silly questions, Cinnamon! There's no such thing as dragons and mermaids. Sing me a wild gypsy song!"

But Cinnamon no longer felt like singing.

Princess Cyprina grew tired of the gypsy princess. "She is a royal bore," she complained to newer companions.

And, truth be told, she was.

That night, Cinnamon tossed and turned upon her soft princess bed. "I am lonely," she cried. "So very lonely."

When at last she fell asleep, she dreamt that her old auntie was searching for her.

"Cinnamon, Cinnamon. Where are you, my child?"

And Cinnamon answered, "I am lost."

The next morning, she scarcely remembered her dream. She knew only that she longed to feel warm earth, not cold marble floor, beneath her feet. At breakfast, she could not eat her pheasant-egg omelet. She asked to be excused.

Princess Cyprina waved her away impatiently.

Cinnamon left the banquet hall and went down to the great gilded gates. Opening them cautiously, she stepped onto the rough road that led away from the palace.

The wind whispered, "Cinnamon, Cinnamon." She wanted to follow, but it was too hard to walk in the high-heeled princess shoes. Cinnamon turned back.

That night, as she tossed and turned upon her soft princess bed, her old auntie again appeared in her dream.

"Who are you, my child?" she demanded.

And Cinnamon answered, "I cannot remember."

The next morning, Cinnamon was more restless than ever. The bars of the palace gates seemed like the bars of a golden cage.

She pushed the great gates open and gazed out into the distance.

"Cinnamon, Cinnamon," the wind whispered.

"The wind is calling to me," she said. She slipped her feet out of the dainty princess shoes and followed the wind over the hills to the edge of a great forest.

There she stopped, afraid to enter. "Oh, my head aches so," she said, touching her golden crown. And she turned back.

That night, once again, her old auntie appeared in her dream. "There are things more precious than a crown of gold," the old gypsy said.

Cinnamon woke up and looked around. She saw nothing — nothing but the wind rippling the water in the fountain outside her window.

The next morning, Cinnamon did not put on her high-heeled princess shoes. She did not put on her golden crown. She did not go to the great hall for breakfast. She went down to the palace gates, opened them wide, and followed the wind.

At the edge of the forest, she stopped and looked back at the palace gleaming in the distance. The wind brushed against her cheek and whispered, "Cinnamon, Cinnamon." And Cinnamon entered the darkness.

Brambles and thorns tore at her dress, but Cinnamon did not turn back. She walked deeper and deeper into the forest. She walked all day and, just as the first stars appeared in the darkening sky, she reached a small lake.

There she rested, ate wild raspberries and slept more soundly, on her bed of leaves, than she had ever slept in her soft princess bed.

She awoke half-expecting to see servants and gilded palace walls. Instead, she saw golden sunshine and a great bear swimming in a cool forest lake.

"Babalatzzi!" Cinnamon cried out joyfully.

Babalatzzi sniffed the air in a puzzled way. He thought he heard his lost friend calling, but he didn't recognize her.

"Grrr!" he growled. Then he turned, swam back to the far shore and disappeared into the depths of the forest.

"Have I changed so much?" Cinnamon wondered, glancing down at her reflection in the clear water. She touched her hair. It felt stiff with pomade and perfume.

"Ugh!" she said, and she dove into the lake. When every last trace of perfume and pomade had been washed away, she rose from the water triumphant. "Babalatzzi may not know who I am, but *I* know who I am.

"I am Cinnamon! I am a gypsy girl! I know how to speak to the wind and…

"...I know how to follow a bear."

She walked all day and did not stop even when the sun set and the moon rose high in the evening sky. She followed Babalatzzi's tracks until, at last, she reached the gypsy camp.

The embers of the campfire were burning low. No one heard or saw her enter. No one, that is, except Babalatzzi. He sniffed the air and growled: "Grrr!"

Cinnamon began to sing softly:

Ba-ba-latzzi! Babalatzzi!
Come and dance a step or two.
Ba-ba-latzzi! Babalatzzi!

And they danced the whole night through!